Praise for Storyshares

"One of the brightest innovators and game-changers in the education industry."
— Forbes

"Your success in applying research-validated practices to promote literacy
serves as a valuable model for other organizations seeking to create
evidence-based literacy programs."
— Library of Congress

"We need powerful social and educational innovation, and Storyshares is
breaking new ground. The organization addresses critical problems facing
our students and teachers. I am excited about the strategies it brings to the
collective work of making sure every student has an equal chance in life."
— Teach For America

"It's the perfect idea. There's really nothing like this. I mean, wow, this will be a
wonderful experience for young people."
— Andrea Davis Pinkney,
Executive Director, Scholastic

"Reading for meaning opens opportunities for a lifetime of learning. Providing
emerging readers with engaging texts that are designed to offer both challeng-
es and support for each individual will improve their lives for years to come.
Storyshares is a wonderful start."
— David Rose, Co-founder of CAST & UDL

Rugs Don't Talk

Storyshares presents

Published by Storyshares, LLC
Inspiring reading with a new kind of book.

The characters and events in this book are fictitious. Any similarity to real persons, living or dead, is entirely coincidental.

Storyshares
Storyshares, LLC
24 N. Bryn Mawr Avenue #340
Bryn Mawr, Pennsylvania 19010-3304
www.storyshares.org

Interest Level: High School
Grade Level Equivalent: 1.6

ISBN 9798885977159
Book design by Saskia Globig

RUGS DON'T TALK

Natasha Lopez

Storyshares

CONTENTS

CHAPTER ONE

Who knew there was a wrong way to shape frybread?

"*Yéigo*!" my *nálí* says.

I sigh, "I can't try any harder, Grandma!"

Kids on TV don't make their own breakfast. Pancakes with gooey syrup are just waiting for them when they wake up.

I smooth out the edges of my dough.

"Is this better?" I ask.

My *nálí* motions to the frying pan with her wrinkled lips.

I toss the dough into the pan. Hot grease splatters all over.

My *nálí* says words in Navajo I'm not allowed to say in English.

"Coo-coo! Coo-coo!" The crusty clock above the door sings.

"I'm late! Bye, Grandma!" I say as I toss my backpack over my shoulder.

"Feed the sheep!" my *nálí* yells.

My *nálí* doesn't know much English. But she says, "Feed the sheep!" perfectly.

I point at the clock. "I'm late!"

My *nálí* places a round piece of frybread in my hand. "Feed the sheep," she says again.

Grandmas on TV say, "I love you," before their grandkids leave for school.

I wonder if "Feed the sheep!" is Navajo for "I love you."

Warm frybread melts on my tongue as I run to the shed.

"What took you so long?" Panda asks.

Panda's real name is Johnny Bitsili. He's got a round head, round eyes, and a round body.

He looks more like a Panda than a Johnny.

I throw a block of hay into the wooden sheep corral. The sheep *baa* happily.

"I failed at frybread lessons again," I explain.

"Making frybread isn't hard. You'll get it," Panda replies.

I dust off my hands. "That's easy for you to say."

"My bread's not *that* good," he says with a smile.

"You're right..." I shove Panda playfully with my shoulder. "Your bread is as tough as mutton compared to my *nálí*'s bread!"

Panda shoves me back. "Your bread probably tastes like manure!"

We chase each other down the dirt road.

CHAPTER TWO

Three scrappy dogs join our run. Panda jumps over a prickly pear cactus.

One of the dogs jumps in front of him at the same time. The dog yips as Panda's foot crushes its tail.

"Careful!" I pull Panda back before he falls into horse manure. Horses along the road throw their heads back, laughing.

"We should walk."

Panda nods his head. "Did you fill out your goals sheet?" he asks.

"No," I reply. "It's dumb. Why are we talking about goals in Culture class? Shouldn't we be making baskets or something?"

"It is kind of dumb..." Panda says quietly.

"What did you write down?" I ask.

Panda twists his hands around his back-pack straps. He looks at the ground. "I... want to be a chef." He quickly adds, "I don't want to be a fancy chef! I could work at the restaurant here."

"You probably could," I reply.

Panda holds his head up high. I think he even skips a little.

"You're smart. I bet you could get into college," Panda says.

I snort. "I don't know about that."

"You gotta dream big! The sky's the limit, dude!"

I hold my hands up to the turquoise sky. My fingers stretch as wide as possible.

No matter how hard I try, the sky doesn't fit into my hands.

I think about the kids on TV. *Does the sky fit in their hands*? I look down at the trailers around me.

Tires weigh the roofs down, so windstorms don't blow them away. Patterned blankets hang over windows to keep cold out.

Rusty old trucks that used to run on miracles are buried in the sand.

"*The sky's the limit*," Panda said.
That might be true, but not here.
All we got here is "Rez life."
That's all I'll ever have.

CHAPTER THREE

"I want to be a *dlanii* when I grow up," Aaron says proudly.

Mr. Tso doesn't blink. "Be serious."

"I am being serious," Aaron replies. "I'll collect tourist tips and drink beer all day. What's better than that?"

Aaron's sidekicks Ray and Everlyn snicker.

Mr. Tso pinches the skin between his eyebrows. "Being a *dlanii* is not a job, and you shouldn't beg tourists for money."

Aaron and Mr. Tso argue back and forth.

I don't know why Mr. Tso bothers. *Dlanii* is probably the best Aaron can do.

I raise my hand.

Mr. Tso turns to me. He still looks annoyed. "Yes, Kai?"

"I have something to say." I turn to look at Aaron. "I support you and your dreams."

Aaron leans back in his chair and laughs like a choking goat. The class laughs with him.

Mr. Tso's arms cross over his chest like an Indian chief in a John Wayne movie.

"What are your goals, Kai?" he asks in a low voice.

I cross my arms like Mr. Tso. "I'm going to be Navajo Nation president."

"Yeah, right!" someone says.

"I mean it! I'm going to make a difference around here. All of you will be begging for my picture!"

Mr. Tso uncrosses his arms. "What kind of changes do you have in mind?"

I slide down in my seat and mumble, "I don't know."

Mr. Tso shakes his head. "I thought so."

CHAPTER FOUR

My face gets hot. "We need more jobs!"

"That's all?" Mr. Tso asks.

I sit up in my seat. "We need more hospitals, too."

Mr. Tso nods his head. "How will you make that happen?"

I go on and on until I notice the class is weirdly quiet. Mr. Tso never smiles, but the corner of his lip turns up a little.

I shut up.

"Anything else?" Mr. Tso asks.

I pause. In my best president voice, I say, "I think alcohol should be legalized on the Reservation!"

Mr. Tso's smile falls into a frown.

"Beers for everyone!" I stand and point at Aaron. Then I point toward the rest of the class. "Beers for you and you and you!"

The class hoots and cheers.

"Quiet!" Mr. Tso's voice disappears behind all the laughter.

"Come on, Mr. Tso!" Aaron grins. "You got to have all the booze you wanted in Phoenix. Let us on the Rez have some fun!"

The bell rings. I grab my books and walk towards the door.

"Stop." Mr. Tso steps in front of me. He's back in his chief pose. "We need to talk."

"Me?" I ask. "What about Aaron?"

"Now," Mr. Tso says sternly.

I can't help myself.

"Yes, Chief," I reply.

CHAPTER FIVE

Mr. Tso sits on his desk. His legs block me from leaving my seat.

"Isn't it illegal to sit on a desk? Do teachers not follow their own rules?" I ask.

"Do you actually want to open more hospitals?" Mr. Tso asks.

"You're going to break the desk," I complain.

Mr. Tso leans in. "Answer my question."

I lean away. "Maybe! I don't know!"

Mr. Tso gets up and digs through some papers on his desk. "How is your *nálí* doing?" he asks.

"She's okay..." I say slowly.

"I heard she hasn't been feeling well," Mr. Tso continues. "Is that the reason why you want to build hospitals?"

Mr. Tso waits for me to reply. My leg shakes.

How long is he going to keep me here?

"I thought I was in trouble?"

"You are." Mr. Tso hands me a detention slip and a packet of paper.

I hold up the packet. "What's this?"

"It's an application for a scholarship to NAU," he replies.

I look from the application to Mr. Tso and back. "Is this part of my punishment?"

"That depends on what you do." Mr. Tso pauses. "You're smart, Kai. But that joke in class wasn't funny."

"The class thought so," I say quietly.

Mr. Tso hears me loud and clear. "See? This is what I'm talking about! You've got a sour attitude!"

A sour attitude? What does that even mean?

"You should take this back, then." I slide the application to him.

Mr. Tso pushes it back.

CHAPTER SIX

"You aren't listening. I said you're smart. Do something with that brain."

I stare at the application. "I can't afford college..."

"That's what the scholarship is for," Mr. Tso replies.

The school bell rings. I shove the application to the bottom of my backpack.

"Wait!" Mr. Tso hands me a note. "Give this to your next teacher, so she knows why you're late."

"Thanks," I reply with no emotion.

Mr. Tso doesn't let go of the note.

"In *Diné Bizaad*," he says.

"*Ahéhee'*," I mumble.

I hide behind some lockers and dig out the wrinkly application. My heart is pounding so loud, but I'm happy. I'm really happy.

And that scares me.

Do the kids on TV feel scared of scholarships?

Do they hold their applications like a feather in a windstorm? Are they afraid their dreams will blow away too?

No. The sky's the limit for them.

For me, this application is all I've got.

CHAPTER SEVEN

"You're such a liar, Curley!" my Aunt Rita says with a smile. Rita holds the phone between her cheek and shoulder while she paints her nails. Her legs swing over the side of the couch.

"You're wasting our phone minutes!" I complain.

Rita ignores me. "I know, Curley. I just work so much. Sometimes, I feel like a bad mom."

"Kai, Kai!" My baby cousin Jolita makes chubby finger guns at me.

We play Cowboys and Indians. Jolita is the cowboy. I'm the Indian. No one ever wants to be the Indian.

"Curley's so weird," I say as Rita hangs up the phone.

Rita blows on her neon-green nails. "You're so weird."

"Why are you dating him?" I ask. "Imagine waking up to his face every morning."

"I'm not *dating* Curley. We're friends."

"That's what you said about Jolita's dad," I mumble.

Rita shoves her toes in my hair.

I push her feet away. "You're so gross!"

"Go help your grandma with her weaving!"

"Okay! Okay!"

CHAPTER EIGHT

I sit on the floor by the wooden loom. White strings of yarn hang from the upper beam. My *nálí* weaves green yarn in between the white. Her weft looks like a prairie dog poking its head in and out of a hole.

"*Łitso*," my *nálí* says.

I hold up some red yarn. "This one?"

"*Łitso*!" She points at the basket of yarn with her lips.

I hold up blue yarn. "Is this right?"

"She wants the yellow yarn, dummy!" Rita picks up the yarn and gives it to my *nálí*.

"I wish grandma spoke English," I complain.

"Mom never went to school. She had to be

with the sheep." Rita rolls her eyes. "What's your excuse?"

"How am I supposed to learn Navajo if Grandma barely talks?" I ask.

My grandpa had been a uranium miner. When he died of lung cancer, my *nálí* stopped singing.

After my parents were killed by a drunk driver, my *nálí* stopped smiling.

Now she only talks if she has to.

"Grandma speaks through her rugs," Rita says.

I snort, "Rugs don't talk."

"Maybe you're not listening."

CHAPTER NINE

Rita holds Jolita on her hip as she stirs the mutton stew. The warm smell makes my stomach growl.

"What are they teaching you in school? Obviously not your colors."

Oh! The scholarship! I almost forgot!

"Be right back!" I say.

I run to my room and pull out the application. Then I run back to the living room. "You think I'm so dumb? Guess who might go to NAU!"

Rita is hunched over the phone with her back turned. Jolita touches Rita's cheek.

"Mommy?"

"Are you sure it's cancer?" Rita's voice shakes.

Suddenly, the mutton stew smells sour.

"I'll write that down..." Rita rushes to put Jolita in her crib. She throws junk on the ground as she searches through drawers.

"Kai, do you have a pen? Oh, never mind!"

Rita grabs her nail polish. She makes a green circle around the 21st day on the calendar.

The nail polish drips like poison.

"Thank you, Doctor. Bye." Rita hangs up.

My nálí.

Jolita and I stare at Rita. Rita doesn't turn around.

Finally, I ask, "Does Grandma have cancer?"

"Could you get some bread from the store?" Rita asks.

"But it's almost dark," I reply.

Rita turns around.

Her eyes speak for her.

My *nálí* has cancer.

CHAPTER TEN

I stop to catch my breath beneath the juniper tree. My fingers dig into the shaggy bark.

Rita said my *nálí* would tell her stories under this tree when she was little. My *nálí* talked about the sweet water she drank growing up. She said it was so good. "*Ayóó łikan*!" she said.

The water was sweet because of the uranium in it. Now my *nálí* has cancer. This stupid tree will live longer than she does.

I scream and kick at the tree. I pull out branches and stomp juniper berries into a chalky paste.

Aaron appears behind the tree. He sways back and forth.

"What's wrong with you?" he asks.

I smell alcohol on his breath.

"I'm fine," I reply.

Aaron looks at the mess I made.

"You sure?" he asks.

I crush pine needles in my hands. "My *nálí* has cancer. Rita works too much. She can't get another job."

"I can get *you* a job," Aaron says.

"You can?" I perk up.

"It's in town. You'll have to miss some school."

"Oh..." I say quietly.

Aaron looks at the branches around us. "I came here looking for wood. A couple of us are having drinks on the hill. You want to join us?"

"No. I want... my *nálí* cured. I want a scholarship." I scream, "I want to get out of the Rez!"

Aaron swats the air. "You worry too much! Come with me."

I don't move.

"You'll feel better. I promise," Aaron says with a sloppy smile.

I sigh. "Fine."

CHAPTER ELEVEN

Aaron and I haul branches up the hill. There are five or six people huddled around a tiny fire.

"It's President Kai!" Ray laughs.

"Ha. Ha," I fake laugh.

I toss wood into the pit and blow on the flame until it grows big.

Everlyn pats me on the back. "Good job, Mr. President!"

"Have a beer to celebrate!" Aaron hands me a 40-ounce beer.

I gulp down the drink.

The group cheers, "Chug! Chug! Chug!"

I gasp for air—my throat burns.

"The first one's the hardest," Aaron says as he hands me another beer.

I drink and drink and drink until I'm like the kids on TV. Up on this hill, we're higher than the moon.

Then I remember my grandma is dying.

I remember we don't have money for chemotherapy.

I remember I have to miss school to work.

I remember this means I won't get into NAU.

"The fire's going out! Anybody got more wood?" Ray asks.

"I do." I pull the scholarship application from my pocket.

Aaron looks at the application. "That's not wood," he says.

"Nope."

I toss the application into the dying flames. My application turns into glowing ashes that float into the darkened turquoise sky.

CHAPTER TWELVE

The Pow Wow is loud with the sound of chanting, drumming, and happy conversations. Families gather on the bleachers to watch dancers in the field.

"Hey, Kai!" Panda wipes frybread flour on his apron. "You want to help me sell some bread? I haven't seen you in forever!"

I look at the crowd. "I've been busy."

Curley appears behind Panda.

"Is Rita here?" he asks.

"Rita's helping my grandma," I reply.

"Oh..." Curley nods his head too many times.

Panda and I wait for him to leave. He doesn't.

"Anything else?" I ask.

Curley looks over my head as he says, "I got Friday off. Tell Rita I can watch her mom while she goes to town."

"Rita's fine. We're fine. Thanks," I reply.

Panda and Curley look surprised.

"Oh. Okay..." Curley wanders away.

"Are you okay?" Panda asks.

"Yeah. Why?" I reply with no emotion.

"Kai! Why didn't you wait for us? Are you embarrassed?" Aaron wraps one arm around my neck.

I smell beer on his breath. Panda's eyes look rounder than usual.

"Look at his face!" Aaron points at Panda. "You look like you've seen a skinwalker!"

Everlyn and Ray laugh. I do too.

"Meet me under the bleachers," Aaron says.

"Sure," I reply.

"Relax, Johnny! I don't bite." Aaron rubs Panda's head and stomps away.

"Why are you hanging out with Aaron?" Panda asks.

I shrug. "He got me a job."

"Is that why you haven't been in school?"

"Relax, Johnny!" I rub Panda's head.

Panda's mouth hangs open. He really looks like he's seen a skinwalker.

I run behind the bleachers before Panda can say anything.

CHAPTER THIRTEEN

"Here." Aaron passes me a drink.

We're like tarantulas in a hole. People look down at us from the bleachers, but they keep their distance.

"Let's dance!" Aaron runs into the field before we can stop him.

Male dancers spin in little circles while hopping on one foot. Aaron spins like a tumbleweed. Female dancers sway delicately. Aaron sways like he's standing on a moving truck.

Do they notice he's drunk?

"*Ya'at'eeh.* I'm Nizhoni," a female dancer says.

I don't recognize her. She must go to another school.

"Why aren't you dancing?" she asks.

"I-I can't dance," I reply.

Nizhoni does the male dance slowly. Her long braids swing with the rainbow-colored fringes of her dress.

I stand there. She repeats the dance.

My feet bounce to the pounding of the drum.

"You got it!" She smiles.

I can't lose that smile.

Chanting echoes in my chest. Colorful dancers surround us. It's like we're dancing in a field of wildflowers after a monsoon rain.

I hear screaming. Everything stops.

Aaron is wrestling on the ground with one of the male dancers. He punches the dancer in the face until two big men pull him off.

"What happened?" I ask Aaron.

"He attacked me!" Aaron spits.

The dancer wipes his bloody mouth. He shakes his head. "You bumped into me! You're drunk!"

"Are you with him?" the big men ask me, Everlyn, and Ray.

I want to say no. I want to dance with Nizhoni.

Aaron answers for me.

"Yeah, so? You gonna arrest us?" he asks.

Security walks up. "You all need to leave."

Ray and I drag Aaron off the field. I look back.

Nizhoni holds her shawl tightly around her chest.

Then, she runs into the dance circle like a feather in a windstorm.

CHAPTER FOURTEEN

"Where were you?" Rita asks.

"Nowhere," I reply.

Rita puts her hands on her hips. "The medicine man just left. Your Grandma kept asking for you."

My *nálí* is sitting by her loom. She's wearing a floral scarf around her head and her best turquoise jewelry.

Why is my nálí dressed like she's going to town?

Baby Jolita cries. Rita picks her up and heads to the bathroom. "I'm not done talking to you! Stay there!" Rita says to me.

"Kai." My *nálí* pats the couch and holds her arms out.

"You need a lift?" I say and put my arms around her.

My *nálí* cries out and pushes me away. She hits the ground with a loud thud.

"Are you okay?" I touch my *nálí*'s arm. She flinches.

Rita runs into the living room. "What did you do?"

"Nothing! I don't know what happened!" I explain.

My *nálí* says something to Rita in Navajo. Rita looks at me with disgust. "Have you been drinking?"

"No," I say quickly.

"She says you smell like beer." Rita runs her hands through her hair. "What are you doing, Kai? You're seventeen! You're ruining your life!"

"My life is already ruined! I have nothing!" I yell.

CHAPTER FIFTEEN

She looks confused. "You have me and your grandma and Jolita."

I scoff. "Jolita's a baby, Grandma never talks, and you're not my mom! Maybe you should try being a better mom to Jolita instead of pretending to be mine!"

Rita steps back. I haven't seen that look on her face since my *nálí* was diagnosed with cancer.

"I should go," I say quietly.

"Don't!" Rita says through tears. "Mom isn't doing well. I don't know how much time she has left."

"I'm sure she'll be fine without me." I head out the door.

"Kai! Wait!" Rita grabs my arm. I shake her off.

"At least say goodbye to your grandma," Rita says quietly.

I turn to my *nálí*. "See you later, Grandma."

My *nálí* stares at me. Her eyes are usually dull because of chemotherapy. Right now, they're brighter than I've ever seen them.

"Feed the sheep," my *nálí* says.

I shake my head. "We don't feed the sheep at night."

"Feed the sheep," she says again.

I pause at the open door for a long time. A cold wind blows inside the warm hogan.

"*Aoo'*. I will," I say.

My *nálí* smiles. She never smiles.

I climb until I'm at the top of the hill. The usual group greets me.

I think about how dressed up my *nálí* was. I think about the smile on her face when she said, "Feed the sheep."

I huddle by the fire. I drink and drink and drink, but I can't stop the cold chill running through my body.

CHAPTER SIXTEEN

Shards of beer glass glitter in the moonlight. They remind me of the New Year's Eve parties I see on TV.

Those kids are in designer clothes and party hats. We're in dusty sneakers and hoodies we've had since middle school.

I laugh to myself.

"What's so funny?" Aaron asks.

"I was thinking about the New Year's Eve parties I see on TV," I reply.

"What's so funny about that?" Aaron asks.

"It's funny how different we look from those kids."

"Because we're not white?" Aaron asks seriously.

My voice cracks, "What?"

Aaron scoffs. "You're always talking about 'kids on TV.' Why? Do you wish you were one of them? You wish you were white?"

"I'm proud of being Navajo," I reply.

Aaron pokes the spot in my chest where my heart is. "You're not Navajo. You're Diné!"

"I know," I say.

"You make me sick!" Aaron paces around the fire. "We got history books and movies telling us we're nothing! We don't need our own people thinking we're nothing too!"

"I don't think that."

"Really? Then why are you here?" Aaron holds up his beer.

"I don't know..." I say quietly.

"You want to know why I drink?" Aaron takes a big gulp of beer. "I get moved from one drunk family member to the next. I don't have a family, but at least I have pride."

My chest feels heavy. It's hard to breathe.

Aaron laughs. "You know what's really funny? Your family loves you, but you act like a sad little orphan just because you didn't get a scholarship."

50

"It's more than that," I say.

"Really?" Aaron gets close. I feel his hot breath on my face. "Your *nálí*'s dying, and where are you?"

I don't respond.

"Where are you?" Aaron screams.

"I think you've had too much to drink." Ray puts a hand on Aaron's shoulder.

Aaron grabs his hand and throws him to the ground. Ray's head hits a rock with a loud crack.

CHAPTER SEVENTEEN

"Ray!" Everlyn screams.

Aaron stands frozen.

I bend down and lift Ray's head.

"He's bleeding!" I cry out.

We hear sirens.

"Cops!" Someone yells. Everyone takes off running like cockroaches in the light.

"Wait! Ray needs help!" I yell.

Aaron throws me his jacket. "Wrap that around his head."

"Help me pick him up," I say.

The sirens scream louder this time. Aaron stops.

"Sorry Kai, you're on your own." Aaron stumbles after the others.

I drag Ray down the hill on my shoulders. I see a white vehicle heading towards us.

"The sirens are from an ambulance, not cops!" I tell Ray. "Hold on."

I set Ray down and run in front of the headlights. The ambulance screeches to a stop.

The driver leans out the window and waves his arm. "Out of the way! We've got an emergency!"

I point to where I left Ray. "My friend's hurt! I need help!"

Paramedics lift Ray into the vehicle. The ambulance makes a turn. Even in the dark, the drive looks familiar. Then I see the Juniper tree.

My body tenses. *It can't be.*

The ambulance stops. Rita waits outside. Her eyes speak for her.

My *nálí* is dead.

CHAPTER EIGHTEEN

I lie under the shade of the Juniper tree.
I wonder how many of my nálí 's stories I'll never hear?

Maybe I should have learned Navajo or how to make frybread.

I should have stayed home that night...
What do I do now?

"I have something for you."

Rita joins me. She rolls out a rug into my lap. "I took this before they burned the house. I just couldn't see this disappear too."

I hold out the rug in front of me. The rug has four sacred mountains on each side.

Right in the middle of the rug is our family. I see Grandpa, Mom, and Dad with the sheep. I see Rita and Jolita playing with some dogs.

Then I see myself. I'm right beside my *nálí* at the loom.

"You were right, Rita," I say quietly. "Rugs do talk."

CHAPTER NINETEEN

Mr. Tso looks over his shoulder. "Another one? What do you want?"

"I want to ask you something," I reply.

Mr. Tso points to a desk. "Sit."

I sit.

"The deadline for the scholarship ended," he says.

"I know," I reply.

"Then, why are you here?"

My words come out quickly. "I want you to teach me Navajo and how to make frybread and how to weave."

"You dropped out of school," Mr. Tso says.

"I'll come back," I reply.

Mr. Tso crosses his arms over his chest. "You never took my class seriously. Why should I let you back in now?"

My head drops. "I'm sorry, sir."

Mr. Tso sighs. "I didn't always live in Phoenix. I grew up on the Mesa."

I hesitate. "You did?"

"Yeah, and I hated it." He frowns. "We had no water, no electricity. Every day all I did was haul water, feed sheep, and chop wood. All I wanted was freedom. So, I moved to Phoenix."

"And you got your freedom?" I ask.

"No," Mr. Tso replies. "I got a job. I got some nice things, but I also got into some trouble. So, I moved back home."

I pause. "But you live in the teacher housing, don't you?"

Mr. Tso nods. "I do. I have an indoor toilet, and I like it that way."

"Why did you move back to the Rez? Why didn't you move somewhere else?" I ask.

"This place doesn't leave you. It'll always be right here." He points to my chest. "I didn't want to run away anymore."

I shake my leg. "I don't want to run away but... I don't want to live here either."

Mr. Tso puts his hands up. "I'm not telling you what to do. You've got to figure that out for yourself. My question is, what do you want right now?"

"I want to get closer to my *nálí*." I lift my head up high. "I want to be proud of who I am."

Mr. Tso grabs his bag and heads to the door.

My head drops.

Mr. Tso stops at the door frame. "Did you and Aaron discuss this?"

"No, why?" I ask.

"He came in before you did. He had a lot to talk about." Mr. Tso crosses his arms. "I told him to come back to class. I hope he does."

"Yeah, me too," I reply.

"I'll see you on Monday, Kai."

I jump out of my seat. "You will?"

"I expect you to be serious this time. Will you?" he asks.

I can't help myself. "Yes, Chief!" I say with a big grin.

About the Author

Natasha Lopez had a chronic case of procrastination when she was growing up. Over time, her symptoms lessened. She was able to complete her first book, *5 Steps to Win Her Heart*, which was one of Storyshares' 2021 contest winners. She was also able to complete *Rugs Don't Talk*, which was a 2022 Storyshares contest finalist. Natasha hopes to continue writing interesting and heartwarming stories for reluctant readers.

About the Publisher

Storyshares is a publisher focused on supporting the millions of teens and adults who struggle with reading by creating a new shelf in the library specifically for them. The ever-growing collection features content that is compelling and culturally relevant for teens and adults, yet still readable at a range of lower reading levels.

Storyshares generates content by engaging deeply with writers, bringing together a community to create this new kind of book. With more intriguing and approachable stories to choose from, the teens and adults who have fallen behind are improving their skills and beginning to discover the joy of reading.
For more information, visit storyshares.org.

Easy to Read. Hard to Put Down.

www.ingramcontent.com/pod-product-compliance
Lightning Source LLC
Chambersburg PA
CBHW071225170626
46809CB00005BA/1944